May 2009

Dear Juana —

I thank you for the friendship
and support you have given
and wanted to share this story
from another place I once called
home.

All the best,

D...

JAMILIA

Chingiz Aïtmatov

# JAMILIA

**TELEGRAM**

London   San Francisco   Beirut

ISBN (10): 1-84659-032-9
ISBN (13): 978-1-84659-032-0

copyright © Chingiz Aïtmatov (*Djamilia*), 1957 and 2007
Translation copyright © James Riordan, 2007

This edition published 2007 by Telegram Books

A full CIP record for this book is available from the British Library
A full CIP record for this book is available from the Library of Congress

Manufactured in Lebanon

**TELEGRAM**

26 Westbourne Grove, London W2 5RH
825 Page Street, Suite 203, Berkeley, California 94710
Tabet Building, Mneimneh Street, Hamra, Beirut
**www.telegrambooks.com**

Here I stand before this little painting in its simple frame. Tomorrow morning I have to go to the village, and I'm gazing long and hard at the painting, hoping it will bring me luck on my journey.

I've never exhibited the picture. What's more, when relatives visit I keep it well out of sight. I'm not ashamed to show it, though it's far from a work of art. It's just that my painting is plain, as plain as the earth depicted in it.

In the background is a patch of bleak autumn sky; the wind is chasing fleeting, piebald clouds over the distant mountain range. In the foreground lies the russet wormwood steppe crossed by a black road still damp from recent rains. Clumps of dry, broken needle-grass grow at the roadside and the footprints of two travellers meander through a muddy wagon track. The tracks fade as the road disappears into the distance. If the travellers were to take another step they would seemingly walk off the canvas. One of them is … But I'm running too far ahead.

It all happened when I was still a young lad, in the third year of the war. The front, round about Kursk or Oriol, was far away, where our brothers and fathers were fighting while we lads of fifteen or so were labouring on the farm. The arduous toil of farming fell upon our slender shoulders; harvest was the toughest time of all. For weeks on end we were away from home, spending days and nights either in the fields, at the threshing shed or on the road delivering grain to the station.

On one such scorching day when it was so hot the scythes burned your hands, I was returning from the station with an empty cart and decided to pop indoors. We lived right next to the river crossing, on a hill where the street ends. Ours was one of a pair of houses enclosed by a thick brick wall; poplars towered above the two homes. For years the two families had been neighbours.

I live in the Big House. I have two brothers, both

older than me, both unmarried, both away at the front and neither had sent any news home for ages.

My father is a carpenter at the farm workshop. After saying his prayers today, he went to work and would not be back until late evening.

My mother and little sister were at home.

Our close relatives live in the house next door or, as it is known in the village, the Little House. It was either our great-grandfathers or our great-great-grandfathers who had been brothers, but I call them close relatives because we all live as one big family. We have kept the tradition going since nomadic times when our forebears used to break camp and round up the sheep together. When collectivization came to the village our fathers built their houses side by side. In fact, at one time the whole of Aral Street, which stretched the length of the village to the middle of the river, consisted of our kinsfolk, all from the same clan.

Shortly after collectivization, the master of the Little House died, leaving a wife and two small sons. We could not abandon a widow and her sons, so our kinsfolk married my father to her. Besides, he was duty-bound to the spirits of his ancestors since he was the deceased's closest relative.

That is how we came to have a second family. We considered the Little House an independent household with its own orchard and livestock, but for all intents and purposes we lived together.

The Little House had also lost two sons to the army: the elder, Sadyk, had left soon after he got married. We had a couple of letters from them, though at lengthy intervals. So the Little House now contained the mother, whom I called *kichi apa* – younger mother, and her daughter-in-law, Sadyk's wife. Both worked on the farm from dawn to dusk. My younger mother was a kind, obliging, inoffensive woman who did her fair share of the work, from digging ditches to watering the fields – in other words, she knew how to handle a hoe, as we say. Fate had blessed her with a hard-working daughter-in-law, Jamilia, who was every bit as industrious as her mother-in-law – tireless and clever, though of quite a different temperament.

I was very fond of Jamilia, and she was fond of me. We were good friends, yet we never dared call each other by our first names. If we had been from different families I would certainly have called her Jamilia; as it was, since she was my eldest brother's wife, I had to call her *jenei*, while she called me *kichine bala* – little boy, though she was not much older than me. It was the custom of the village for a woman to call her husband's younger brother *kichine bala*.

My mother managed both households aided by my little sister, a funny little lass with ribbons in her plaits. I shall never forget how hard she worked in those difficult days. It was my sister who took the lambs and calves of both houses to pasture; she was the one who collected dung and firewood to keep the homes supplied with fuel. She was the one, my little snub-nosed sister, who brightened my mother's lonely days, distracting her from gloomy thoughts of her sons reported missing in action.

Our large family owed its state of harmonious plenty to my mother. She was the sole mistress of both households, the custodian of the family home. She was quite a young girl when she entered the family of our nomadic grandfathers and she always revered their memory, ruling the families justly. She took charge of everything in the house, and the villagers treated her as the most respected, conscientious and wise person they had. To tell the truth, the village never regarded my father as the family head. I would often hear folk say, 'If I were you, I wouldn't go to *ustaka* (that's our term of respect for a craftsman), all he knows is his axe. Their senior mother is head of the household; you'd do better going to her.'

I have to say that despite my few years I frequently interfered in our household affairs. I could do so because my elder brothers had gone off to war. More often in jest, but sometimes in all seriousness, I was called the *jigit* of the two families, the protector and breadwinner. I was proud of that and felt a deep sense of responsibility. Besides, my mother encouraged my independence; she wanted me to be smart and self-assured, not like my father who spent his days planing and sawing, never speaking to anyone.

So there I was one day, stopping the cart at the house in the willow's shade. I had loosened the traces and was heading for the yard when I spied Orozmat, our team chief, sitting on his horse as usual, with his crutch tied to the saddle. My mother was standing alongside, disputing something or other. As I came closer I heard my mother say, 'Certainly not. Heaven help us if a woman should cart sacks about. No, my friend, you leave my daughter-in-law alone, let her continue as she is. I hardly see light of day any more, you try to run two households. It's a good thing my girl's big enough to lend a hand now. I haven't been able to straighten my back for weeks, it hurts as if I've been bent over mat-making, and then there's the corn gasping for water.'

She spoke testily, while tucking the end of her turban under her collar, always a sign she was cross.

'What's got into you?' muttered Orozmat, lurching in the saddle. 'If I had a good leg and not this stump, d'you think I'd ever ask? Why, I'd much prefer to toss the sacks in the cart myself and race those horses like I used to. I know it's not women's work, but where the hell am I to get the men? That's why we have to use soldiers' wives. You may not want your daughter-in-law to go, but we have the authorities on our backs. The soldiers need food and we're upsetting the plan, and that won't do, will it?'

I came up to them, dragging my whip along the

ground, and as the team chief noticed me he suddenly brightened, evidently struck by an idea.

'Well, if you're that frightened for Jamilia,' he said cheerily, pointing to me, 'I'm sure her little brother will keep an eye on her. Have no fear, Seit's a good lad. It's boys like him, our breadwinners, who are seeing us through these days.'

Mother did not let him finish.

'Good gracious, just look at you, you scallywag,' she shouted at me. 'Your head's all overgrown with weeds; a fine father we have, not finding time to shave his son's head for him.'

'Well then, let the lad stay home with his parents today,' said Orozmat, supporting my mother. 'Seit, you stay home and feed the horses, then we'll give Jamilia a cart tomorrow morning, and you'll pitch in together. Mind you, you'll be responsible for her. Don't you fret, *baibiche*, Seit'll take good care of her. For that matter I'll send Daniyar along too. You know him, he's harmless enough, just invalided out of the army. The three of them can cart grain to the station, then who'd dare lay a hand on Jamilia? That's true, isn't it, Seit? What do you think? We want to make Jamilia a driver, but your mother won't hear of it. You try to persuade her.'

I was flattered by the man's praise; he had consulted me as he would a grown man. Besides, I quickly thought, how pleasant it would be to go to the station with Jamilia. Putting on a grave face, I said to my mother, 'No harm will come to her, you don't think the wolves will get her, do you?'

And casually spitting through my teeth like a seasoned driver, I sauntered off, dragging the whip behind me.

'Hark at him,' my mother exclaimed, half pleased, yet at once she retorted angrily, 'I'll give you wolves, you smart aleck.'

'Well, he should know,' said Orozmat taking my side. 'He's your *jigit* for two families, you should be proud of him.'

He glanced at her anxiously, lest she turn nasty again. But my mother, making no objection, suddenly turned morose and, heaving a sigh, muttered, 'He's still a child, far from being a *jigit*, though granted he's on the go day and night. God knows what's become of our dear *jigits;* our homes are as empty as winter pastures.

I was just out of earshot, so I couldn't hear what she said after that. I was whipping up a cloud of dust as I strode towards the door and I ignored my little sister's welcoming smile. She was busy making cakes of dung for fuel, slapping them from one hand to the other. At the doorway I squatted down and languidly washed my hands with water from the pitcher. Then I went in, drank a bowl of sour milk and stood by the window, crumbling bread into a second bowl of milk.

Mother and Orozmat were still in the yard, but they were no longer arguing. They were talking in calm, quiet voices, probably speaking of my brothers. I could tell that by the way Mother kept wiping her eyes on her sleeve, nodding absently at his words. He was evidently trying to comfort her as she gazed far into the distance, way above the treetops, as though her misty eyes could see her sons somewhere out there.

Lost in her grief, she seemed to have resigned herself to his proposal and he, satisfied at having got his way, was urging his horse out of the yard. Needless to say, neither I nor my mother realized then where all this would lead.

I had no doubt that Jamilia could cope with a

two-horse cart; she was good with horses. After all, she was the daughter of a horse-breeder from the hill village of Bakair. Our Sadyk was once a horse-breeder and one spring had a race with Jamilia and, folk say, failed to beat her. Who knows whether it was true or not, but folk also say that subsequently the ashamed Sadyk had kidnapped her. Others said it was a love match. Be that as it may, they had only lived together for four months before war broke out and he was called up.

I don't know why, but there was something manly about her, a harshness and, at times, even crudeness. Perhaps it was because from childhood Jamilia had herded horses with her father and, being his only child, she was both son and daughter to him. She worked doggedly, with a man's temperament. She got along all right with the other women, but if anyone treated her unjustly, she would swear like a trooper; it was not unknown for her to grab someone by the hair the odd time.

More than once neighbours had been in to complain. 'What kind of a daughter-in-law is that?' they'd say, 'She's only been in your house a moment and already she's pushing her weight around. No respect, no shame.'

'Good job too,' my mother would say. 'Our Jamilia calls a spade a spade. That's better than being two-faced and underhand. Your girls act as if butter wouldn't melt in their mouths, but it's rancid butter: all smooth and golden on the outside, but rotten inside.'

Father and our younger mother never treated Jamilia as coldly as in-laws are supposed to; they were kind to her, they loved her, their only desire being that she was faithful to God and to her husband.

I understood them. Having seen four sons off to war, they found consolation in Jamilia, the only daughter-in-law of the two households, that's why they respected her. What I couldn't understand was my own mother; she wasn't the sort of person who would show her feelings for someone. She was domineering and stern, living by her own rules and never budging an inch. For instance, every spring she pitched the old nomad tent my father had made as a lad in the yard, and burned juniper wood inside it to appease the spirits. She brought us up to work hard and respect our elders; and she demanded absolute obedience from every member of the family.

Right from the outset, however, it was clear Jamilia was not the accepted kind of daughter-in-law. True enough, she respected her elders and obeyed them, yet she never shrank before them, nor did she go gossiping behind their backs like the other girls used to. She was not afraid to speak her mind. Mother often agreed with her, though it was Mother who invariably had the last word.

I think she saw in Jamilia's frank and fair ways a person equal to herself and dreamed of one day making her mistress of the house. My mother saw her as powerful a custodian of the household as herself.

'Praise be to Allah, my daughter,' Mother would say, 'that you've come into a strong and blessed house. That's your good fortune. A woman's happiness is to have children and live in a house of plenty. And one day you'll have, thank the Lord, all we old folks have acquired. We can't take it with us to the grave. Happiness, though, belongs to those who retain their honour and conscience. Mark my words.'

There was something about Jamilia that bothered her in-laws; she was too high-spirited, just like a little child. At times she would have a fit of giggles for no reason at all, and laugh so noisily and happily. When she got home from work, instead of coming straight indoors, she would race about the yard and leap over the ditch. Or for no apparent reason she would kiss and hug first one mother-in-law, then the other.

And another thing: she loved to sing, she was always humming some tune, not shy of people hearing. All this, of course, was not the village way of how a daughter-in-law should conduct herself. But both her mothers-in-law would console each other – she would surely simmer down with time, hadn't they all been like that as girls? As for me, she was the most wonderful person in the world. We had such fun together, giggling at nothing and chasing each other round the yard.

Jamilia was quite pretty. Tall and graceful, with straight, coarse hair tied in two tight, heavy plaits. She used to wear her white headscarf at an angle on her brow. It was very becoming and accentuated her dark skin and smooth features. Whenever she laughed, her bluish-black, almond-shaped eyes would light up mischievously, and whenever she sang a saucy village ditty, a knowing twinkle would appear in her beautiful eyes.

I often noticed that the young men, especially those home on leave, were much taken by her. She enjoyed a joke along with the rest of them, but she was always quick to check anyone who tried to take liberties with her. All the same, it did get on my nerves at times. I was jealous, as younger brothers are of their sisters, and if I noticed young men hanging round her, I would try to get rid of them. I'd puff myself up and give them a fierce look, as if to say, 'Watch your step, she's my brother's wife, so don't think there's no one to protect her.'

I would butt into the conversation to ridicule her suitors, and when that failed I'd lose my temper and stalk off in a huff.

The young men would have a good laugh.

'My, my, just look at him. Surely she can't be his *jenei*. What a joke!'

I tried to control myself, but my ears would burn and tears of hurt would well up in my eyes. Jamilia, my *jenei*, would understand. Barely able to restrain the merriment bubbling up inside her, she'd put on a serious face and tell the men straight, 'So you think I am yours for the asking, do you? Maybe that's how it is where you come from, but not here. Come on *kaini*, pay no heed.'

And strutting before them, she would give her head a haughty shake and shrug her shoulders, smiling quietly to herself as she led me away.

I could see both annoyance and pleasure in the smile; she was probably thinking, 'You stupid boy, if I wanted to do as I fancy there'd be no holding me. The whole family could spy on me and it'd make no difference.' At such times I would keep a guilty silence. True enough, I was jealous of her, I worshipped her, I was proud of her being my *jenei*, of her beauty, independence and reckiess nature. She and I were bosom pals and kept no secrets from each other.

The village had few men in those days. Taking advantage of the situation, the remaining young fellows would behave quite insolently and treat the women with disdain, as if to say, 'Why bother if all you have to do is click your fingers and they come running?'

Once, during harvest, a distant relative called

Osman tried to get fresh with Jamilia when she was resting in the shade of a haystack. He was the type who thought no woman could resist him. But she pushed him away roughly and jumped up.

'Hands off,' she muttered angrily, turning away. 'What can one expect from young rams like you?'

As Osman lay sprawling beneath the haystack, his moist lips curled in a sneer, 'A cat will spurn the cream before it. Why play so hard to get? I bet you're dying for it, why be so choosy?'

She spun round. 'Maybe I am. But that's how things are, you can laugh all you like, you swine. I'd be a soldier's widow for a hundred years and still wouldn't waste my spit on the likes of you. You make me sick. If it weren't for the war I'd like to see who'd even bother with you.'

'That's what I say,' said Osman with a smirk. 'It's wartime and you're dying for your husband's whip. If you were my wife, girl, you'd sing a different tune.'

Jamilia was about to give him a piece of her mind, but she had second thoughts; he wasn't worth it. Instead she threw a long, hateful look at him, spat in disgust, picked up her pitchfork and stalked off.

All that time I was on the other side of the haystack and, when she saw me, she turned away sharply, realizing how I must be feeling. I felt it was me, not her, who had borne the insult, the disgrace.

'Why bother with such people?' I reproached her. 'Why even talk to them?'

Jamilia went about the rest of the day with a look as black as thunder; she did not utter a word to me and did not smile once. When I drove the cart up, she swung her pitchfork into the hay, hoisted it up and carried it in front of her face, preventing me from seeing the pain she was trying to conceal. She tossed the hay into the cart and swung about abruptly for another load. Soon the cart was full. As I drove off I turned round and saw her leaning dejectedly on the fork handle for a few minutes, lost in thought, before pulling herself together and getting back to work.

By the time we had loaded the last cart Jamilia seemed to have driven the incident from her mind and she stood for a while looking at the sunset. There, beyond the river, at the very margin of the Kazakh steppe the harvest sun of evening was blazing like the mouth of a burning *tandyr*. It sank slowly below the horizon, tinting loose clouds with purple hues and casting dwindling rays upon the mauve steppe which was shaded in the hollows with the indigo of early twilight. Jamilia was gazing at the sunset enraptured, as if witnessing a miracle. Her face was aglow with tenderness, her lips parted in a gentle smile, just like a child's. Then, all at once, as if in response to my unspoken reproaches, she turned and murmured in a tone that assumed a continuation of our conversation, 'Don't give him a thought, *kichine bala*, the rat. He's not worth it.'

She fell silent, her gaze sweeping over the fading horizon; then, with a sigh, she continued pensively, 'How could someone like Osman know what's in a person's soul? Nobody knows. Maybe no man in the world knows what's in a woman's soul.'

While I was busy swinging the horses about, she had dashed off to a woman working to one side and I could hear their boisterous, happy voices. It is hard to say what had brought the change in her – perhaps the sunset had lit up her soul or she was simply glad to get the work over and done with. I was sitting in the cart, on a big pile of hay, watching her tear off her white headscarf and chase after a girlfriend through the shadows of the stubble, her arms flung open wide, the breeze flapping the hem of her frock. And my sadness lifted too.

That chatterbox Osman isn't worth worrying about, I told myself, whipping up the horses, 'Giddy-up.'

That day, as the team chief had said, I waited for my father to come home to shave my head; in the meantime I began a letter to my brother Sadyk. Even in this we had our conventions: my brothers wrote letters to my father, the village postman handed them to my mother, and it was my duty to read and answer them. Before opening the letter I knew exactly what Sadyk had written. All his letters were the same, as alike as two lambs in a flock. He would invariably start with the words 'Wishing you good health' before going on, 'I'm sending this letter by post to my family residing in fragrant, blossoming Taras, to my dearly beloved, esteemed father Jolchubai …' Then he would greet the rest of us in strict sequence, starting with my mother, then his mother. After that would follow questions about the health and well-being of the village *aksakals,* the honoured elders of our clan and close relatives, and only right at the end, as if in afterthought, he would add, 'and give my regards to my wife Jamilia'.

Naturally, when one's father and mother are alive, when the village is full of *aksakals* and close relatives, it is awkward, even improper to mention one's wife first, let alone write a letter to her alone. Every self-respecting man knew that. It was never questioned, it was the village custom, and far from being open to debate, we never even stopped to ask whether it was right or not. Besides, every letter was a long-awaited, joyful event in the family.

Mother would make me read the letter several times. Then, with pious reverence, she would hold it in her chapped hands, as if the page were a bird about to fly away. Painfully bending her stiff fingers she would finally fold the letter back into a triangle.

'Oh, my dear boys, we shall preserve your letters like lucky charms,' she would murmur in a voice quivering with tears. 'He's asking how father, mother and the family are – whatever will become of us? We're all here in the village. But how are things with you out there? Just one little word to say you're alive, that's all we need, no more.'

Mother would sit gazing at the triangle for ages before putting it into a leather case where she kept all the letters, and then she would lock it away in a trunk.

If Jamilia happened to be home at the time she was permitted to read the letter. Each time she picked it up I noticed how she blushed; she would read it to herself, greedily, her eyes racing over the lines. But as she read on, her shoulders sagged lower and lower, with each line the colour faded from her cheeks. With brows knitted in a stubborn frown she would leave the final lines unread and return the letter to Mother with such cold indifference, as if returning a borrowed pot.

Mother evidently understood her feelings and did what she could to cheer her up.

'Come on,' she'd say, locking the trunk. 'You should be happy, not down in the dumps. You're not the only one whose husband's gone off to war, you know. You're not alone in your suffering – everyone's the same, bear up with the rest. Do you think there are those who aren't lonely, who don't miss their husbands?

You grieve, my girl, but don't let it show, keep it to yourself.'

Jamilia would say nothing, yet her stubborn, miserable look seemed to say, 'You don't understand, Mother.'

This time Sadyk's letter had come from Saratov where he was in hospital. He wrote that, God willing, he would be back home on convalescence by autumn. This was the second time he had told us and we were all looking forward to his homecoming.

I did not stay home that day, I drove off to the threshing shed where I usually spent the night. First I took the horses to the lucerne meadow and hobbled them; the farm manager would not let us graze the animals on lucerne, but to keep the horses fit I broke the rules. I knew a secluded spot in a hollow and, anyway, no one would notice anything amiss at night. This time, however, as I was unhitching the horses and setting them to graze I noticed that someone had already left four horses there. That annoyed me. After all, I was in charge of the two-horse cart, so I had every right to be indignant. Without a moment's thought I decided to chase away the horses and teach a lesson to the fellow who had invaded my territory. All at once, I spotted a pair belonging to Daniyar, that same fellow the team chief had mentioned earlier that day. Since he and I were to work together the next day, taking grain to the station, I left the horses alone and went back to the shed.

Daniyar was already there. He had just finished oiling the wheels of his cart and now was tightening the axle nuts.

'Daniyar, are those your horses in the hollow?' I asked.

He slowly turned his head.

'Two are mine.'

'And the other pair?'

'They belong to whatshername, Jamilia, is it? She's something to do with you, isn't she, your *jenei*?'

'That's right,' I said.

'The team boss left them here and told me to keep an eye on them.'

A good job I hadn't chased them off!

Night fell and as the evening breeze from the hills settled down for the night, things in the shed settled down too. Daniyar lay down beside me under a pile of straw, but soon after got up and walked down to the river. He stopped at the edge of the bank, and stood there, his hands behind his back, his head tilted to one side. With his back to me, his long, angular figure sharply outlined in the soft moonlight looked as if it was hewn from the landscape. He seemed to be listening to the sound of the river rapids growing louder with the coming of night. Or maybe it was some nocturnal murmuring beckoning him.

'I bet he's going to spend the night by the river; he's a queer one,' I thought to myself with a grin.

Daniyar had only recently come to the village. One day at haymaking a boy had run up to say there was a wounded soldier in the village, though he didn't know his name or where he was from. What a rumpus that caused. Whenever a man returned from the front, every person, young and old, would run to take a look at the newcomer, shake his hand and ask him if he had seen anyone from their family or heard any news. That time the hubbub was unimaginable, each of us wondering whether it was our brother or brother-in-law coming back. So all the haymakers raced back to the village to find out.

It turned out that Daniyar, the unknown soldier, was originally from our village. Orphaned at an early age, he was passed from house to house for three years before finally going to the Chakmak steppe to live with Kazakhs who were kinsfolk on his mother's side. The boy had no close relatives in the village to claim him back, so he was soon forgotten. When people asked him about his life after leaving the village, he was evasive; yet it was clear he had had his full share of woe and knew what it was to be an orphan. He had been like a rolling stone, moving from one place to another. For some time he had herded sheep in the Chakmak salt marshes, and when he was older he had dug canals in the desert, worked on the new cotton farms and then in the Angren mines near Tashkent, from where he had joined the army.

People were glad he had returned to his native village, saying, 'No matter how far he's wandered, he's come back home, which means it's his fate to drink water from his native ditch. Nor has he forgotten his native tongue, he has a bit of a Kazakh accent, but he's fluent enough.'

'Tulpar, the legendary steed, will find his own herd

even at the ends of the earth,' our *aksakals* said. 'Whose land and people aren't dear to one's heart? Good for him to return to us. We are content and so are the spirits of our ancestors. And now, God willing, we'll finish off the Germans and live in peace and Daniyar will raise a family like the rest of us, his own smoke will rise from his hearth.'

By invoking Daniyar's ancestors they were saying he was one of us. And that is how a new kinsman appeared in our village.

Later, Orozmat brought this tall, stooping soldier with the stiff left leg to our hayfield. With his greatcoat slung over his shoulder, he limped along trying to keep up with Orozmat's trotting horse. Alongside the tall Daniyar, our short, bouncing team chief resembled a restless river snipe and it made us laugh.

Daniyar's gammy leg took a while to heal, he could not bend it at all, so he was no good as a mower; he was assigned to tend the mowing machines with us boys. To be honest, we weren't all that keen on him. First his reserved manner irked us, he said so little, and when he did speak you sensed he was thinking of something else, something distant. He had his own thoughts, you never knew whether he saw you or not, even though he'd be looking straight at you with those dreamer's eyes.

'Poor devil, you can see he hasn't recovered from the war,' we used to say of him.

Strangely enough, considering he always seemed to be in another world, he was a quick and skilful worker. If you didn't know him well you might have thought him unsociable. Perhaps his tough childhood had taught him to hide his thoughts and emotions, had made him so withdrawn. Who knows?

Daniyar's thin lips with their hard lines at the corners were always shut tight, his eyes were sad and wistful, and only his lively, mobile eyebrows gave life to his drawn, world-weary face. Sometimes he would give a start as if hearing something inaudible to the rest of us, then his eyebrows twitched and his eyes glowed with a strange rapture. He'd give a long smile and brighten up for some unknown reason. It all seemed most odd to us. But that wasn't all. He had other peculiarities as well. Of an evening we would unhitch our horses and gather round the tent, waiting for the cook to make supper, but Daniyar would climb the old look-out hill and sit there until dark.

'What on earth's he up to, standing guard or something?' we would laugh.

Once, out of curiosity, I crept up the hill behind him. There was nothing out of the ordinary: the lilac-coloured steppe stretching far into the foothills and the dark, dim fields slowly melting into the still night.

He took no notice of my presence; he just sat there, hugging his knees and gazing into the distance with a pensive, yet unclouded look. And once again I felt he was listening intently to sounds I could not hear. Now and again he would shudder and freeze, his eyes open wide. Something was bothering him and I fancied he would get up at any moment and unburden his soul, but not to me – he didn't even notice me – rather to something vast, unbounded, unfathomable. I would stare and not recognize him as he sat there, hunched and melancholy, as if he was just resting after the day's work.

The hayfields of our farm are scattered along the floodlands of the Kurkureu River. Nearby the river bursts out of a gorge and rushes down the valley in an unbridled, raging torrent. Haymaking coincides with the annual flooding of the mountain rivers. Towards evening the muddy, foaming water would begin to rise and round about midnight the river's mighty shuddering would wake me as I slept in the tent. Stars in the calm blue sky would peep into the tent: a cold gusty breeze would blow as the earth slept and the raging river bore menacingly down on us. We were not right by the riverbank, yet at night the water sounded so close, I was often stricken with panic by the thought of the tent being swept away. Meanwhile my friends slept like a log and I, being restless, would go outside.

Night-time in the Kurkureu floodlands is beautiful and awe inspiring. Here and there you can spot dark shapes of the hobbled horses in the meadow; having eaten their fill of dewy grass, they doze warily, occasionally letting out a snort. Nearby the Kurkureu hollowly rolls its pebbles along, bending the dripping, windswept rose-willows. The restless river fills the night with eerie, awesome sounds. Terrifying.

My thoughts always turned to Daniyar on such nights. He used to sleep in a stack of hay at the river's edge. Wasn't he scared? Didn't the crash of the river deafen him? Did he get any sleep? Why did he spend his nights alone on the bank? What force drew him there? A strange fellow, it was almost as if he really was from another world. Where was he now? I glanced about me but could see no one. The banks receded into distant sloping hills, and the mountain range loomed eerily in the gloom. Up there, on the summits, all was still and starlit.

You would have thought Daniyar could have made friends in the village by now, yet he kept to himself as ever, as if he shunned friendship or enmity, affection or envy. In a village, a man who can stand up for himself and others, who is capable of doing good and sometimes even wrong, who knows how to handle himself at a feast or a wake without bowing to the *aksakals,* is generally acclaimed by all men and noticed by the women.

But if a person who, like Daniyar, keeps to himself and takes no part in the village's everyday affairs, then he will simply be ignored by some, while others will say condescendingly, 'He does no harm nor good to anyone. Let him be, poor soul, he'll survive.'

Such a loner is normally the butt of all jokes or an object of pity. And we teenagers, who always wanted to appear older than we were, to match true *jigits*, would always be laughing at Daniyar behind his back – not daring to do so to his face. We even laughed at him washing his army shirt in the river; he'd rinse it out and put it on while it was still wet, for he had no other.

The funny thing was that although he was mild and reserved, we were never really friendly with him. Not because he was older than us – what difference did three or four years make? That would not have stopped us from being familiar. And he was not at all stern or conceited, which can sometimes lose a person respect. No, there was something inaccessible in his silent, brooding manner that restrained us, even though we liked to poke fun.

I used to be an inquisitive little pest and frequently annoyed people with my ceaseless questions; my real passion was to ask ex-soldiers about the war. Of course, when Daniyar came to work with us, I kept waiting for my chance to learn something from him.

After work one evening we were sitting round

the fire, eating and taking it easy, and I asked him, 'Daniyar, tell us about the war before we bed down for the night.'

He said nothing for a while, even seemed put out by the question, staring hard into the fire; then he looked up and glared at us.

'Talk about the war?' he asked, as if responding to his own private thoughts. 'No, it's better to know nothing about it.'

Then he turned his head, scooped up a handful of dry leaves, tossed them on the fire and blew on them without looking at us. He said no more. We realized from that short retort that war was not a subject you could talk about lightly, it was no bedtime story. The war had formed a hard clot deep in the man's heart and it was hard for him to talk about it. I felt ashamed of myself and never questioned him about it again.

However, the evening was soon forgotten, just as quickly as the village lost interest in Daniyar himself.

So there we were, Daniyar and I, spending the night together in the threshing shed. Early next morning, as he and I led the horses in, Jamilia arrived. As soon as she spotted us, she shouted, 'Hey *kichine bala*, come on, bring me my horses. Where's the harness?'

And she began to inspect the carts closely as though she had been a driver all her life, kicking the wheels to see if the bushing was firm.

As we drove up she must have found us an amusing sight. Daniyar's thin, lanky legs dangled inside a pair of wide tarpaulin boots that looked as if they were about to slip off at any moment, and I, with bare, black, filthy heels, urged on the horse by kicking its flanks.

'What a pair,' she cried, tossing her head gaily. And straightaway she began ordering us about, saying, 'Hurry up, we have to cross the steppe before it gets too hot.'

She seized the bridle, led the horses to the cart and set to hitching them up. She managed it too, asking me only once to show her how to adjust the reins. She ignored Daniyar, as if he were not there. He was evidently taken aback by her self-assurance and determination. He stood staring at her with an unfriendly look, yet with barely concealed admiration, his lips shut tight. As he silently lifted a sack of grain from the scales and carried it to the cart, Jamilia set upon him. 'That won't do, we all have to pitch in, we can't go working by ourselves. Right, fellow, give me your hand. Hey, *kichine bala,* what are you gawking at, get into the cart and stack the sacks.'

She grabbed Daniyar's hand and the poor fellow blushed from embarrassment as they hoisted a sack on crossed hands. And every time they carried a sack, grasping each other's wrists tightly, their heads nearly touching, I saw how terribly ill at ease he was, how nervously he bit his lip, how he tried to avoid Jamilia's face. Jamilia, though, was not the least concerned, hardly noticing her helper, exchanging jokes with the woman at the scales. Then, when the carts were loaded and we had taken up the reins, she turned to him, winking slyly and chuckling, 'Hey you, what's your name, Daniyar is it? Since you look like a man you might as well lead the way.'

Daniyar jerked the reins, silent all the while, and we were off.

You poor soul, I thought. To cap it all, you're bashful too.

The journey ahead was a long one, a score or more kilometres over the steppe, then down through the ravine to the station. The only good thing was that it was all downhill and easy on the horses. Our village lies on the bank of the river, on the slopes of the Great Mountains, so you can see its dark treetops all the way to the ravine.

We made only one trip a day, leaving early in the morning and making the station a little after midday. The sun beat down mercilessly and the station was packed. It was hard to get through, what with carts and waggons from all over the valley piled high with sacks, as well as mules and bullocks bringing loads from the distant hill farms. They were driven by young lads and soldiers in shabby tunics, burnt black by the sun, their bare feet raw from the stony roads, their lips cracked until they bled from the heat and the dust.

A canvas sign hung upon the grain elevator: 'Every Kernel of Grain for the War Effort'. The confusion, jostling and raucous shouting of the drivers in the yard was indescribable. Behind a low fence nearby, a railway engine was manoeuvring into position, gushing sudden clouds of hot steam and reeking of burning clinker. Trains passed through with a deafening roar. Camels, reluctant to get up, bellowed in fury and frustration, their slavering jaws opening wide.

The mountains of grain at the receiving centre were piled high beneath a baking hot tin roof; the sacks had to be carried up sloping planks right under the roof and the air was heavy with the smell of grain and choking dust.

'Hey you, watch what you're doing,' shouted the receiving agent from below, his eyes red from lack of sleep. 'Take them to the top, as high as you can go.' And he shook his fist and cursed irritably.

What was he cursing for? We knew where to take them; that's where we were going anyway. After all, we were carting this grain on our shoulders all the way from the field where old men, women and children had sown and reaped it. At the height of harvesting the combine operator had struggled with the antiquated machine, women were forever bent over their scorching scythes and children nimbly retrieved every dropped kernel of grain.

I still remember just how heavy those sacks were that we carried upon our backs. It was a job for the hardiest of men. I would stagger up the slope, balancing on the creaking, sagging planks, my teeth holding on to a corner of the sack to prevent it falling. Dust tickled my throat, my ribs ached with the weight, and I'd see stars dancing before my eyes. Many a time I'd get dizzy half-way up, feeling the sack sliding off my back and I'd wish I could chuck it off and go tumbling down with it. But there were others behind me carrying sacks, they were lads of my own age or soldiers' wives who had children just like me. If it hadn't been for the war we wouldn't have been allowed to bear such a load. No, I had no right to give way when women were doing the same work.

Jamilia walked ahead of me, her skirt tucked up above her knees; I could see the taut muscles straining on her lovely tanned legs and the effort it took to hold her lithe body steady as she bent under the weight of the sack. Occasionally, she halted for a split second, sensing that I was weakening with every step.

'Keep it up, *kichine bala*, we're almost there,' she'd say. But her voice was cracked and hollow.

When we had emptied our sacks and turned back, we saw Daniyar coming up. He limped slightly as he walked in his firm, measured step up the planks, alone and taciturn as ever. As we came abreast of him he gave Jamilia a black, searing look, but she ignored him, flexing her aching back and puffing down her creased dress. Each time he looked at her it was as if he were seeing her for the first time, but she continued to ignore him.

It set into a pattern: either she laughed at him or ignored him completely. It all depended on her mood. We'd be riding along the road when something got into her and she'd let out a shout, 'Aida, let's go.' With a whoop, and swinging the whip above her head, she set the horses into a gallop; and I followed. We'd overtake Daniyar, enveloping him in thick clouds of dust that took a long time to settle. Though she did it in jest, few men would have put up with it. Daniyar, though, didn't seem to mind. We'd thunder by while he looked on with grim admiration at the giggling Jamilia standing up in her cart. As I turned back I'd see him peering at her through the dust. And there was something kindly, all-forgiving in his look, yet I sensed also a stubborn, secret yearning.

Neither the mocking, nor the utter indifference ever caused him to lose his temper; it was as if he had vowed to bear it all. Initially I felt sorry for him and more than once I said to Jamilia, 'Why poke fun at him, *jenei*, when he's so meek and mild?'

'It won't do him any harm,' she laughed. 'I just do it for a joke, he's such a lone wolf anyway.'

It was not long before I too started to tease him as much as she did. His strange, obstinate looks began to get under my skin. How he would stare as she hoisted a sack upon her back. True enough, amidst all that noise and bustle of the market-place, with folk hoarse from yelling and fussing, Jamilia's precise movements and light step caught the eye, as if it were all happening in some other time and space.

You couldn't help staring at her. To fetch a sack from inside the cart, she would have to stretch up and bend, thrust her shoulder forward and toss her head back in a way that bared her pretty neck and made her sun-kissed plaits almost touch the ground. Daniyar would pretend to take a breather, his gaze following her to the door. He probably thought no one noticed, but I did, and I didn't like it. I even took offence since I reckoned Daniyar thoroughly unworthy of her. Just think, even he has his eye on her, I'd fume.

The childish egotism I had not yet outgrown

flared up inside me in terrific jealousy. Children, after all, always resent their loved ones associating with outsiders. And instead of pity for him I felt an intense dislike which made me enjoy it when others poked fun at him.

One day, however, our jokes backfired. Among the grain sacks we were taking to the station was an extra-heavy one weighing 140 kilos, sewn from coarse, raw wool. Usually all of us carried it together since it was far too heavy for one person. But that day at the threshing shed we decided to play a trick on Daniyar. We dumped the heavy sack into his cart and piled the other sacks on top. On the way to the station Jamilia and I stopped off at a Russian village to pick some apples from an orchard, and we giggled the rest of the way. Jamilia even lobbed apples at Daniyar; then, as usual, we overtook him, kicking up clouds of dust. But he caught up with us at the railway crossing on the other side of the ravine because the boom was down. From there to the station we drove along together. We had completely forgotten about the heavy sack and did not give it a thought until we had finished unloading. Jamilia gave me a crafty dig in the ribs, nodding towards Daniyar. He was standing beside his cart, staring puzzled at the sack, apparently wondering what to do with it. Just then he whipped round and caught Jamilia hiding a smile; at once he realized what was going on and blushed a deep red.

'Hitch your pants up or you'll lose them on the way!' shouted Jamilia.

He threw us a furious look and, before we had time to move, he tugged the sack along the cart bottom, set it on the edge, jumped down and, holding it steady with one hand, hoisted it on to his back. At first we pretended there was nothing special about it; no one else noticed anything out of the ordinary – there was a fellow carrying a sack like everybody else. But as he reached the gangway Jamilia overtook him.

'Let go of the sack, I was only joking,' she hissed.

'Clear off,' he muttered, stepping on to the plank.

'Look, he's carrying it!' Jamilia cried, as if trying to justify herself. She still laughed softly, but her laughter had become somewhat forced.

We noticed that he was beginning to limp quite markedly with his wounded leg. Why hadn't we thought of that earlier? Even now I cannot forgive myself for that stupid trick.

'Come back,' Jamilia shouted through hollow laughter. But he could not turn back; people were close behind him.

I don't even remember exactly what happened next. I saw Daniyar bent double under the enormous sack, his head bowed low, his teeth biting his lip. He was moving slowly, carefully shifting his bad leg. Each fresh step was obviously causing him such pain that his head jerked back and he would halt for a second. The higher he climbed up the plank, the more he swayed; it was the sack which swung him from side to side. My throat went dry from fear and I felt ashamed. Frozen with terror, every fibre of my body felt the weight of his burden and the unbearable pain in his wounded leg. Again he lurched, his head jerked back, but by then my head began to swim, everything went black and the earth whirled beneath my feet.

I was woken by a sudden steely grip upon my arm. I did not recognize Jamilia immediately. She was as white as a sheet, her huge pupils dilated in her wildly staring eyes, her lips still twitching from recent laughter. By now everyone else, including the agent, had rushed to the foot of the gangway. Daniyar took a couple more steps, tried to adjust the sack and then slowly began to sink to one knee. Jamilia covered her face.

'Let go. Let go of the sack,' she cried.

But for some reason he would not, even though he could certainly have let it slip over the side to avoid knocking over those behind him. At the sound of her voice he lurched forward, straightened his leg, took another step and lurched once more.

'Let go, you stupid bastard,' yelled the agent.

'Let go,' people were shouting.

But he stood his ground.

'No, he's not going to let go,' someone murmured with finality.

Everybody present, those behind on the plank and those below, seemed to realize he would not let go of the sack unless he fell with it himself. A deathly hush fell upon the crowd. We could hear the engine outside whistling shrilly.

Swaying like a drunk, Daniyar moved up the sagging boards of the gangway towards the scorching hot tin roof. After a couple of steps he stopped to regain his balance and gather strength to continue upwards. Those behind fell in step and halted whenever he did. It tired them out, drained their last ounce of strength, yet no one lost their temper, no one cursed him. They walked as if their loads were tied together by an invisible rope, as if treading a dangerous slippery path, where the life of one depended on the life of another. A dull, monotonous rhythm throbbed in their concerted silence and unison swaying. One step, then another, men keeping step with Daniyar.

Only a short distance remained, the gangway incline would soon come to an end. But he stumbled again, his bad leg no longer obeying him; surely he would fall if he kept hold of the sack.

'Run and give him a hand from behind,' Jamilia shouted to me, desperately holding out her arms as if to help him.

I dashed up the gangway, elbowing my way through people and sacks, and finally reached him. He shot me a glance from under his arm. The veins were throbbing on his dark, wet brow and his bloodshot eyes burned through me with hate. I wanted to support the sack from behind, but he hissed at me, 'Clear off.' And he inched his way forward to the top.

When at last he came down, gasping and limping, his arms dangling by his sides, people parted to let him by, but the agent could not control his relief.

'Are you mad, fellow? I'm human too, you know, you could have emptied that sack down here. What do you have to go carrying such sacks for?'

'That's my affair,' Daniyar replied softly.

Spitting to one side, he moved towards the cart. We did not dare look up. We were ashamed and furious that he had taken our foolish trick so seriously.

All through the night we rode along in silence. Since that was Daniyar's natural state we could not tell whether he was still annoyed at us or whether he had forgotten the entire incident. We, however, were conscience-stricken and felt wretched.

Next morning, as we were loading sacks at the threshing shed, Jamilia took hold of the ill-fated empty sack, stepped firmly on one edge and ripped it apart.

'Here, take your old rag,' she cried, tossing the sack at the surprised weighing woman's feet. 'And tell the team chief not to dump such sacks on us next time.'

'What's got into you?' the woman asked.

All next day Daniyar concealed his hurt, behaving as calmly as ever, though his limp was worse. Yesterday's incident had evidently reopened his wound; it was a constant reminder to us of our guilt. It would have been easier if he had laughed or joked; that would have put an end to our disagreement.

Jamilia pretended that nothing unusual had occurred. She laughed as haughtily as ever, but I could see she was ill at ease all day.

It was late as we returned from the station. Daniyar was riding ahead of us. It was a wonderful August night: the glittering stars were so clearly visible, they seemed closer than they really were. One star sparkled with icy rays as if rimmed in hoar-frost, and looked down from the dark sky at us, blinking in innocent bewilderment. I followed it for a long time as we rode through the ravine. Eager to reach home, the horses trotted briskly, the stones scraping beneath their feet. The cool wind from the steppe brought with it the bitter pollen of flowering wormwood, and the faint aroma of ripening wheat. Mingling with the smell of tar and horse sweat, it all made us faintly dizzy.

Dark rocks overhung with briar towered over the road, while far below the irrepressible Kurkureu gushed out from behind a thicket of rose-willow and wild poplar. Now and then a train chattered over a distant bridge behind us, the tapping of its wheels echoing long after it had passed.

It felt good to ride along in the coolness of night, to watch the jogging backs of the horses, to listen to the sounds of the August night and inhale its odours. Jamilia was riding ahead of me; she had let the reins drop and was humming softly as she looked about her. I understood: our silence hung heavily upon her. It was a night for singing.

So she sang. Perhaps she sang because she wanted somehow to recall the former easy spirit of our relationship with Daniyar or she wished to assuage her feeling of guilt. Her voice was clear and impassioned as she sang the usual village songs: 'I'll wave my silken scarf to you' and 'My loved one is far away'. She knew a lot of songs and sang simply, with feeling. It was a pleasure to listen to her.

All at once she broke off and called to Daniyar,

'Hey you, Daniyar, how about a song? Are you a *jigit* or not?'

'You sing, Jamilia, you sing,' he called back, embarrassed, reining in his horses. 'I'm listening, I'm all ears.'

'Don't you think we have ears too?' she shouted. 'Nobody's forcing you, you know.'

And she struck up a song again. Who knows why she asked him to sing. Perhaps just for the fun of it or maybe she wanted to draw him into conversation? Probably she wanted to talk to him.

A few minutes later she yelled again, 'Tell me, have you ever been in love?'

Then she burst out laughing. He said nothing. Jamilia fell silent too.

She's picked the right one for a song, I sniggered to myself.

The horses slowed as they forded a stream that crossed the road; their hoofs clattered on the wet silvery stones. When we had passed through, Daniyar urged his horses on and unexpectedly began to sing in a strained voice that jumped at every bump in the road.

'Mountains mine, bluey-white mountains,
Land of my fathers and my kin.'

He suddenly faltered, coughed, but sang the next two lines in a deep, slightly hoarse voice,

'Mountains mine, bluey-white mountains,
Cradle of mine …'

Here he broke off again as though afraid, and fell silent.

I could well imagine how confused he must have been. Yet even in that halting, timid singing there was something singularly moving. He certainly had a fine voice, it was hard to believe it really was him.

'Well I never,' I exclaimed.

Jamilia cried out, 'Where have you been all this time? Go on, sing, sing properly.'

Ahead, at the ravine's exit, the light of day was creeping in and a breeze came from the valley. Daniyar began to sing again. He started off as timidly and uncertainly as before, yet steadily his voice gained volume, filling the ravine and echoing in the distant rocks.

I was astounded at the passion and fire of the melody itself. I could not describe it then, nor can I now. Was it just his voice or something more tangible emerging from his very soul that could arouse such emotion in another person, and bring one's innermost thoughts to life?

If only I could recreate his song. It contained few words, yet even without words it revealed a great human soul. I have never heard such singing before or since. The tune was like neither Kirgiz nor Kazakh, yet in it was something of both. His music combined the very best melodies of the two related peoples and had woven them into a single, unrepeatable song. It was a song of the mountains and the steppe, first soaring up into the sky like the Kirgiz mountains, then rolling freely like the Kazakh steppe.

I listened in amazement. So that's what he's like, I thought. Who would have thought it?

As we crossed the steppe along the soft, beaten track, Daniyar's singing took wing; songs followed one another with astonishing facility. Was he really so gifted? What had happened to him? It was as if he had been saving himself for this very day. His hour had come at last.

And all of a sudden I began to understand his strangeness that made people shrug and mock; his dreaminess, his love of solitude, his silent manner. Now I understood why he sat on the look-out hill of an evening and why he spent a night by himself on the riverbank, why he constantly hearkened to sounds others could not hear and why his eyes would suddenly gleam and his drawn eyebrows twitch. He was a man deeply in love. I felt it was not simply a love for another person, it was somehow an uncommon, expansive love for life and earth. He had kept this love within himself, in his music, in his very being. A person with no feeling, no matter how good his voice, could never have sung like that.

When you thought the last note had died away, out burst a fresh, haunting song that seemed to rouse and caress the sleeping steppe with tunes it held dear and, in return, gratefully invigorated the singer. The ripened dove-grey wheat awaiting harvest rippled like a lake surface and the first shadows of dawn flitted across the field. At the mill a mighty throng of old willows rustled their leaves;

on the other side of the river the campfires of field-workers were fading, and a shadowy rider galloped noiselessly towards the village along the top of the bank, dipping and bobbing among the orchards. The wind was heady with the fragrance of apples, the aroma of honeyed, flowering corn and the warm smell of drying dung bricks.

Daniyar sang on oblivious to all about him. The enraptured August night listened to him in silence. Even the horses had long since switched to a measured walk, as if afraid to break the spell.

Abruptly, on the highest, ringing note, he broke off and, with a whoop, urged his horses into a gallop. I thought Jamilia would race after him and I half prepared to follow, but she did not stir. She was sitting with her head inclined, and remained in that position as if still catching the last tremulous notes drifting on the air. Daniyar had ridden off, yet neither of us said a word until we had reached the village. Words were not necessary; besides, words can never quite express a person's feelings.

Something changed in our lives that day. Every morning we'd load our carts at the threshing shed, go to the station and be off again as fast as we could in order to hear Daniyar's songs on the return journey.

As for me, his voice seemed to dog my every step. It was with me every morning while I ran across the wet lucerne field to the hobbled horses, as the laughing sun slid out from behind the hills to greet me. I heard his voice in the soft rustling of golden wheat as it was tossed up into the wind by the old winnowers, and in the solitary kite flying gracefully high above the steppe. I saw and heard his music in everything.

In the evening, as we rode through the ravine, I felt I was being transported to a different world. I listened to Daniyar with my eyes half closed, and before me flashed strangely familiar scenes from childhood. First the delicate, smokey-blue, migratory spring clouds floating at crane's height above the *yurtas;* then herds of horses racing across the ringing earth, neighing and pounding to their summer pastures, the young stallions with streaming forelocks and wild, black fire in their eyes proudly overtaking their mares; then flocks of sheep slowly spreading like lava over the foothills; now a waterfall gushing from the rocks with blinding, creamy-white, foaming water; the sun setting calmly in the thicket of needle-grass beyond the river, and the solitary distant rider on the horizon's fiery margin dashing in pursuit – surely all he had to do was stretch out his hand and touch the sun and he too would vanish into the thickets and twilight.

The Kazakh steppe is broad beyond the river. It had shoved our mountains aside and now lay there forbidding and desolate.

In that first memorable summer when war began, fires flared across the steppe, herds of army horses obscured it in hot dusty clouds and riders were forever galloping in all directions.

I recall a mounted Kazakh on the opposite bank shouting out in a shepherd's guttural tones, 'Saddle your horses, Kirgiz, the enemy's at hand.' And he rushed on into the waves of heat haze, leaving clouds of dust billowing in his wake.

Our first cavalry regiments moved down from the hills and through the valleys in a solemn bleak rumble. Thousands of stirrups jangled, thousands of *jigits* headed into the steppe, red banners waved from the colour staffs before them, while beyond the dust kicked up by the horses' hooves came the mournful, majestic wailing of wives and mothers.

'May the steppe give you strength. May the spirit of our warrior *Manas* protect you.'

Bitter traces remained where the men had gone off to war.

Daniyar's singing had opened my eyes to this world of earthly beauty and anguish. Where had he learned it? Whom had he heard it from? I realized that only someone who had yearned for and endured love for his native land could love it so. As he sang I could see him as a boy wandering the paths of the steppe; perhaps it was then that the songs had awakened in his soul. Or was it when he had trod the fiery paths of war?

His singing made me want to fall to the ground and kiss it, as a son to a mother, grateful that someone could love it so keenly. For the first time in my life something new awoke within me, something irresistible: I still cannot explain it. It was a need to express myself, yes, to express myself, not only to see and sense the world, but to bring to others my vision, my thoughts and sensations, to describe the beauty of the earth as inspiringly as Daniyar could sing. I caught my breath for fear and joy of the unknown. At that time, however, I had not yet realized the need to take up brush and paints.

I had always enjoyed drawing. I used to copy pictures from textbooks and my classmates would say they were perfect copies. Teachers at school used to praise my drawings in our school paper. But when war broke out and my brothers were called up I left school and went to work on the farm like all my friends. I forgot all about paints and brushes and never thought I'd remember them. But Daniyar's singing had stirred my soul and I went about in a daze, looking at the world through bewildered eyes, as though I were seeing everything for the first time.

And how Jamilia had changed. It was as if the witty, sharp-tongued giggler had never existed. A glowing springtime yearning now clouded her eyes; she was forever lost in thought during our journeys, and a vague dreamy smile would play upon her lips as she quietly rejoiced at something only she was aware of. Many a time when she hoisted a sack on her back she would just stand there, gripped by an inexplicable timidity, as if facing a raging torrent, not knowing whether to cross it or not. She avoided Daniyar, averting her gaze.

Once at the threshing shed she told him with helpless, tormented frustration in her voice, 'Why don't you take off your shirt, I'll give it a wash.'

Afterwards, when she had washed it in the river, she laid it out to dry and sat beside it, painstakingly smoothing out the creases, holding the worn shoulders up to the sun, shaking her head and then stroking it again, quietly and wistfully.

Only once did she give a loud, infectious laugh and her eyes shone brightly as before. A noisy crowd of girls, young women and invalided *jigits* called in at the shed on their way home from stacking hay.

'Hey, *bais,* you're not the only ones to fancy white bread,' the young men called. 'Give us some or we'll chuck you into the river.'

And they thrust their pitchforks at us in jest.

'Your pitchforks don't scare us,' replied Jamilia gaily. 'I'll gladly treat the girls, but you men can fend for yourselves.'

'Right, into the water with them,' shouted the men.

And the young men and women wrestled playfully; with shouts and squeals and chuckles, they tried to shove each other into the water.

'Grab them, fling them in,' Jamilia laughed loudest of all, neatly and nimbly side-stepping her attackers.

The funny thing was that the *jigits* had eyes only for Jamilia, each one trying to grab her and press her close. All at once three young men had hold of her and were carrying her to the bank.

'Give us a kiss or we'll throw you in,' they shouted. 'Come on, let's give her a swing.'

She writhed and wriggled, calling to her girlfriends for help, but they were running madly up and down the bank trying to fish their scarves out of the water. To the happy laughter of the men Jamilia flew into the water with a splash. She emerged with her hair streaming water, more lovely than ever. Her wet cotton frock clung to her body, outlining her strong round hips and young breasts, but she was blithely unaware of it, laughing, swaying to and fro as merry streams of water coursed down her flushed face.

'Give us a kiss,' the men persisted.

She did so, but she was still thrown into the water

and again came out laughing, tossing back the heavy wet strands of hair from her face.

Everyone at the threshing shed was laughing at the young people's games. The old winnowers set aside their spades and wiped tears from their eyes; the wrinkles on their dark faces shone with joy and the fleeting spirit of youth revived. I too laughed heartily, having for once forgotten my jealous duty to protect her from the *jigits*. Only Daniyar was silent. By chance I caught a glimpse of him and broke off laughing at once. He was standing alone at the edge of the threshing floor, his feet planted wide apart. I felt that he would have liked to have rushed forward to snatch her away from the young men, but he just stared at her with a look of sadness and admiration; joy mingled with pain. Yes, Jamilia's beauty was a source of joy and grief to him. While the young men were pressing her close and forcing her to kiss each in turn, Daniyar looked down at his boots and made as if to leave. But he remained.

Meanwhile, Jamilia had noticed him too; she stopped laughing at once and hung her head.

'That's enough fooling about for one day,' she said abruptly, checking the boisterous men.

One was still trying to put his arms around her, but she shoved him back, tossed her head and stole a guilty glance at Daniyar before running into the bushes to wring out her frock.

I was not at all clear about their relationship, and if the truth be known I was afraid to dwell on it. Yet I did feel uneasy whenever I saw her miserable. It would have been better if she had laughed and poked fun at him as before. At the same time, our trips back home at night to the sound of his singing filled me with a strange sense of indescribable happiness for the two of them.

Jamilia used to ride in the cart when we drove through the ravine, but she would walk alongside it when we crossed the steppe; I would too, for it was more pleasant to walk and listen to the singing. At first both of us followed our own cart, though it was not long before some strange force drew us closer and closer to Daniyar; we wanted to see the expression on his face and in his eyes. Surely the person singing was not the unsociable, melancholy Daniyar we all knew?

Each time I observed that Jamilia, entranced and moved almost to tears, would slowly stretch out her hand towards him, but he seemed not to see it. He would be gazing upwards at something far away, his hands behind his head, swaying from side to side, and her hand would drop helplessly to the side of the cart. She would give a shudder, pull her hand away sharply and come to a halt. Then she would stand in the centre of the road, downcast and stunned, gazing after him for a long while before moving on.

At times I felt both Jamilia and I were troubled by the same, equally unfathomable emotion. Perhaps it had lain hidden deep in our souls and had only now come to life?

She was still able to lose herself in the work, yet she could find no rest even in those rare moments of distraction as we hung round the shed. She would give the winnowers a hand, tossing a few shovels of wheat high in the air, then suddenly she would throw aside her shovel and walk over to the bales of straw.

There she sat in the shade and, as if afraid of being alone, she'd call to me, 'Come here, *kichine bala*, let's take a rest.'

I always expected her to tell me something important, perhaps explaining what it was that troubled her. But she did not. Silently laying my head in her lap, she gazed into the distance, ruffling my bristly hair and gently stroking my face with trembling, hot fingers. I would look up at her, at her face so full of vague anxiety and yearning, and I seemed to recognize myself in it. She too was assailed by something that was gathering and maturing in her soul, seeking an outlet. And she was plainly frightened by it. Simultaneously she painfully wished and did not wish to admit to herself that she was in love, in the same way as I was keen and not keen for her to love Daniyar. After all, she was my family's daughter-in-law, my brother's wife.

But such thoughts were only fleeting. I drove them away. My greatest joy was to see her tender lips half parted as a child's, to see her eyes misty with tears. How fine and lovely she was, what bright animation and passion filled her face. Even now I often ask myself if love produces a feeling akin to that experienced by an artist or poet. Gazing at Jamilia I so wanted to run away into the steppe and cry out, asking heaven and earth what I should do to suppress that inexplicable anxiety and that inexplicable joy that I felt. One day I think I found the answer.

We were returning from the station as usual. Night had already fallen and stars were swarming in little clusters up in the sky. The steppe was dropping off to sleep and only Daniyar's song pierced the stillness, ringing out and fading in the soft distant darkness. Jamilia and I followed on behind.

I don't know what came over Daniyar that night, there was such a tender, penetrating, yearning loneliness in his singing that it brought tears of compassion and sympathy to my eyes. Jamilia was walking alongside his cart, her head to one side, holding on tightly to the edge of the cart. And as his voice began to soar again, she tossed her head, sprang into the cart and sat down beside him. She sat there as if turned to stone, her hands folded across her chest. I was walking alongside, hurrying forward to have a better look at them. He continued singing, seeming not to notice her beside him. I saw her arms drop weakly to her sides and her head lightly rest upon his shoulder as she leaned towards him. Just for a moment, like a horse changing step under the whip, his voice wavered, then rang out with even greater power. He was singing of love.

I was stunned. The steppe seemed to burst into

bloom, heaving a sigh and drawing aside the veil of darkness, and I saw two lovers in its vast expanse. They did not seem to notice me, it was as if I was not there. I was walking along and watching as they, oblivious to the world, swayed together in tune with the song. And I did not recognize them. It was the same old Daniyar in his shabby army shirt unbuttoned at the throat, but his eyes seemed to gleam in the gloom. It was my Jamilia clinging to him, yet so quiet and timid, with teardrops sparkling upon her eyelashes. They were newly born, uniquely happy people. Was this not true happiness? Was not Daniyar giving this inspired music utterly to her, was he not singing for her, singing about her?

Once more I was overcome by that indescribable excitement which Daniyar's singing always aroused in me. And all of a sudden I knew clearly what I wanted: I wanted to draw them.

My thoughts scared me. Yet the wish was stronger than the fear. I would draw them exactly as they were: happy. Yes, exactly as they were right then. Would I be able to do it? I held my breath in fear and joy. I was walking along as if in a trance. I too was happy, for

I was not to know what pain this rash desire would cause me in the future. I told myself you had to see the earth as Daniyar saw it, then I would relate his song in paints, and I too would have mountains, steppe, people, grass, clouds and rivers. The thought even occurred to me, But where would I get the paints? School wouldn't give me any. They needed them themselves. As if that was the major problem.

Daniyar's song ended abruptly. Suddenly Jamilia threw her arms around his neck, then instantly drew back. Just for a moment she was motionless, then she leapt down from the cart. Daniyar tugged hesitantly at the reins to stop the horses, but she was standing in the road with her back to him.

Then she gave a toss of her head, glanced at him sideways and, barely able to contain her tears, said, 'What are you looking at?' After a moment, she added harshly, 'Don't stare at me, get going.' And moving to her cart, she set on me, 'What are you gaping at? Get in and pick up the reins. You make me sick.'

What on earth had come over her? I wondered, urging on the horses.

It was not hard to guess. It certainly was not easy

for her, what with a lawful wedded husband lying in a Saratov hospital. But I had no desire to delve into that. I was so angry at her and myself. I could have hated her had it not been for fear of not hearing Daniyar sing again, of never hearing his voice.

A terrible weariness racked my body, I could not wait to get back and tumble into the hay. The backs of the horses jogged up and down in the dark, the cart rattled unbearably and the reins kept slipping from my grasp.

Back at the shed I unfastened the horse collar with some difficulty and threw it under the cart before collapsing in the hay and falling asleep. This time Daniyar led the horses out to graze.

Next morning, though, I awoke with joy in my heart. I was going to draw Jamilia and Daniyar. I shut my eyes tight and imagined precisely how I would portray them; all I needed was to pick up a pencil and start sketching.

I ran down to the river to wash and as I dashed over to the hobbled horses, the cool, wet lucerne slapped against my bare legs, stinging and cutting the skin on my feet. But it felt wonderful. As I ran along I drank in the scene around me. The sun was peeping out from behind the hills and a sunflower that had somehow sprung up by the ditch was reaching towards it. White-crowned knapweed crowded it greedily, yet the sunflower stood firm, catching the morning sun with its yellow tongues and nourishing its tight, heavy basket of seeds. Over there at the ditch crossing water trickled down the waggon tracks where the wheels had churned up the mire. And to one side lay a lavender island of fragrant, waist-high mint. Here was I racing over my native soil as swallows swooped overhead – oh, if only I had the paints to capture the morning sun, the blue-white mountains, the dew-drenched lucerne and the solitary sunflower growing by the ditch.

When I returned to the shed, my joyful mood evaporated instantly. I caught sight of a sullen, drawn Jamilia; she looked as though she had not slept a wink all night. Dark shadows lay beneath her eyes.

She neither smiled nor spoke to me, but the moment Orozmat appeared she went up to him and said brusquely, 'You can take your cart back. Send who you like, but I'm not going to the station again.'

'What's up, Jamilia, been bitten by a horsefly?' he said jokingly.

'Hold your tongue!' she snapped. 'I said I won't, that's that.'

The smile faded from his face.

'Like it or not, you'll carry grain,' he said, banging his crutch on the ground. 'If someone's offended you, speak up and I'll break this crutch over his head. If not, don't mess me about: it's the army's bread you're delivering, you own husband's.'

Turning sharply, he hobbled away on his crutch.

Jamilia went red, darted a glance at Daniyar and sighed. He was standing to one side with his back to her, jerkily tightening the hames of the horse's collar. He had overheard the entire conversation. For a while Jamilia stood where she was, fingering her whip, then she gave a careless shrug and walked towards the cart.

That day we returned earlier than usual. Daniyar raced his horses all the way, while Jamilia sat silently gloomy; I could hardly believe it was the scorched and blackened steppe lying before us. Why, only yesterday it had all been so different. It was as if I had just heard about it in a fairy tale and I could not get the picture of happiness out of my head. I had seemingly grasped the brightest outline of life, imagining it in every detail. I would not rest until I had stolen a sheet of white paper from the weigher. I ran off with it and hid behind a haystack; there, with thumping heart, I laid the paper on the smooth wooden spade which I had taken from the winnowers on the way.

'The Blessing of Allah upon it,' I murmured, as my father had once done when setting me on a horse for the first time. Then I touched the paper with my pencil. Those were my first untutored lines. Yet when Daniyar's features appeared on the paper I forgot about everything. I imagined the nocturnal August steppe lying upon the paper, and myself listening to Daniyar singing with his head thrown back and his chest bare; Jamilia was clinging to his shoulder. It was my very first independent picture: the cart; the pair of them, the reins thrown over the headboard; the horses' backs bobbing in the darkness; and the steppe and distant stars in the background.

I was so engrossed in my drawing that I was oblivious to everything around me. I only snapped out of it when I heard a voice right above me say 'Are you deaf?'

It was Jamilia.

Blushing, with no time to hide the sketch, I hung my head in shame.

'The carts are all loaded and this past hour we've been shouting for you all over. What on earth are you doing here? And what's this?' she asked, picking up my drawing. 'Hm?' she said, angrily shrugging her shoulders.

I wished the ground would open up and swallow me. She stared long and hard at the sketch, then looked up at me with moist, anguished eyes.

'Let me have it, *kichine bala*,' she said quietly. 'I'll put it away as a keepsake.'

Folding it in two she tucked it inside her blouse.

We were soon on the road and I found it hard to return to reality. It all seemed a dream. I could not believe I had drawn something that resembled what I had witnessed. Yet somewhere deep inside me welled up a naïve feeling of triumph, even of pride; and dreams – each more daring than the next, each more enticing – made my head swim. At that moment I wanted to make a host of pictures, but with paints instead of a pencil. I was unaware of how fast we were travelling; it was Daniyar who was racing his horses and Jamilia trying to keep up with him. She kept glancing about her, occasionally smiling in a touching, guilty way. It made me smile too, for it meant she was no longer cross with us, and if she were to ask, Daniyar would surely sing again that night.

We arrived at the station that day much earlier than usual, with the horses in a lather. The carts had scarcely halted before Daniyar began unloading the sacks. Goodness knows why he was in such a hurry and what had come over him. Whenever trains passed, he'd stop and follow them with a long, thoughtful gaze. Jamilia also glanced in that direction in an effort to understand what was on his mind.

'Come over here, the horse-shoe's loose,' she suddenly called to him. 'Help me get it off.'

As soon as Daniyar had prised off the shoe held steady between his knees, and straightened up, she looked into his eyes and said softly, 'Don't you care or understand? Am I the only one who does?'

He silently averted his gaze.

'Do you think it's easy for me?' she sighed.

His eyebrows twitched and he gazed at her with love and sorrow, muttering something that I did not catch. Then he quickly walked to his own cart, looking satisfied. He was stroking the horse-shoe as he went. Watching him I wondered what comfort he could have found in Jamilia's words. How could a person find comfort in another's heartfelt sighing and in such words as 'Do you think it's easy for me?'

We had finished unloading and were ready to leave when a wounded soldier entered the yard, a gaunt figure in a crumpled greatcoat, with his kitbag slung over one shoulder. He had arrived on the train that had pulled in a few minutes earlier; now he glanced about him and shouted, 'Is anyone here from Kurkureu?'

'I am,' I replied, wondering who it could be.

'Who are you, son?' the soldier asked, coming towards me. But straightaway he spotted Jamilia and a happy grin spread across his face.

'Kerim, is that you?' she cried.

'Jamilia, little sister,' cried the soldier, running towards her and squeezing her hand tightly in his.

It turned out to be a fellow villager.

'Well, well, what luck,' he said excitedly. 'I've just come from Sadyk, we were in hospital together. God willing, he'll be home himself in a couple of months. As I left I told him to write his wife a letter, I said I'd take it. Here it is, signed and sealed.'

Kerim handed her a triangular army envelope.

Jamilia seized the letter, turned red then white, and glanced warily at Daniyar. He stood alone beside the cart, feet planted wide apart, his eyes full of despair as he stared at her.

By then people were running from all over. The soldier recognized friends and relatives in the crowd; he was bombarded with questions. Before Jamilia had a chance to thank him for the letter, Daniyar's cart had dattered by and flew out of the yard, leaving a cloud of dust as it bumped along the rutted road.

'He must be crazy,' people shouted.

The soldier had gone off, leaving Jamilia and me standing in the centre of the yard, gazing after the fast disappearing cloud of dust.

'Come on, *jenei*,' I said.

'You go on, leave me here,' she said heatedly.

For the first time each of us rode back alone. The

stifling heat scorched my parched lips. The earth, cracked and seared, had grown white from the heat of day. It seemed to be cooling down, covered with salty grey flakes. The sun, quivering and shapeless, shimmered in the salty, whitish haze. Above the dim horizon, orange-red storm clouds gathered; gusts of dry wind covered the horse muzzles with white dust and swept their manes back as it passed by, then continued on to ripple clumps of wormwood on the hillsides.

'Are we going to have rain?' I wondered.

How lonely I felt, what anguish oppressed me. I urged on my horses as they strained to slow to a walking pace. Frightened, spindly bustards scampered off into the gully. Withered leaves of desert burdock swept along the road – but we have no burdock around here, it must have blown over from the Kazakh side. The sun had set and not a soul was in sight, only the day-weary steppe.

It was dark when I reached the threshing shed. The air was still and windless. I called to Daniyar.

'He's down by the river,' answered the watchman. 'It's so humid, everyone's gone home; you can't work at the shed with no wind.'

I chased the horses out to graze and decided to head down to the river; I knew Daniyar's favourite spot above the overhang. He was sitting there, hunched over, his head resting on his knees, listening to the rushing water below. I would have liked to have gone up to him, put my arm around him and said something comforting. But what would I say? After standing there for a while I finally turned around. I lay on the hay for a time, looking up at the cloud-darkened sky and wondering why life was so incomprehensible and complicated.

Jamilia was still not back. Where had she wandered? Even though I was dead beat I could not sleep; I could see lightning flashes in the cloud banks above the hills.

I was still awake when Daniyar returned to the threshing shed. He wandered about aimlessly, keeping a watchful eye on the road. Finally he collapsed behind a bale of straw upon the hay alongside me. I felt sure that he would abandon us, that he would no longer stay in the village. But where would he go? Alone and homeless, he had nobody to go to. As I was dozing off

I heard the slow clatter of an approaching cart; it must be Jamilia coming back.

I don't remember how long I had slept when I felt the straw rustle by my ear and someone pass by, like a wet wing lightly brushing my shoulder. I opened my eyes. It was Jamilia. She had come from the river in her cool, damp dress. She stopped, glanced round anxiously, and sat down beside Daniyar.

'Daniyar, I've come, I came of my own accord,' she said softly.

All was silence. A bolt of lightning slid down the sky noiselessly.

'Are you cross? Are you very angry?'

Silence again, then the faint splash of a clod of soil slipping into the water.

'It isn't really my fault,' she whispered. 'Nor yours.'

Thunder rumbled far over the hills. Jamilia was plainly silhouetted in a flash of lightning. She glanced round and dropped down beside him, her shoulders heaving convulsively in his arms. She stretched out on the hay and pressed against him.

A broken wind rushed in from the steppe, whirled the straw about, buffeted a dilapidated tent that stood outside the shed and spun off like a crazy top down the road. Once again there came a dry crash of thunder breaking overhead and blue flashes piercing the storm clouds; it was both terrifying and exciting – the storm was bearing down on us, the last storm of the summer.

'Surely you didn't think I would swap him for you?' she whispered hoarsely. 'No, no, no. He never loved me, he even sent his regards as a postscript. I don't need his tardy love and I don't care what people say. My lonely darling, I'll never let you go. I've loved you for so long. Even when I did not know I loved you, I was waiting for you, and you came as if you knew I was waiting.'

Light blue lightning flashes repeatedly plunged jaggedly over the river by the overhang and slanting fresh raindrops began to patter upon the straw.

'Jamiliam, Jamaltai,' murmured Daniyar, calling her by the tenderest Kazakh and Kirgiz names. 'Turn round and let me gaze into your eyes.'

The storm broke. The felt covering was wrenched off the tent and flapped about like a stricken bird. The rain, whipped up by the wind, lashed down in raging torrents as though it were kissing the earth in passion. Mighty peals of thunder rolled across the heavens and bright flashes of summer lightning lit up the hills as brightly as a spring field of tulips, while the wind howled and raged in the ravine.

The rain came down and I lay there buried in the hay, feeling my heart thumping in my breast. I was happy. I felt that I had emerged into the sunshine for the first time after a long illness. Even though the rain and the lightning flashes reached me beneath the hay I was content and fell asleep with a smile upon my face, uncertain whether the sound I heard was Daniyar and Jamilia whispering or the subsiding rain pattering on the straw.

The rains had come and summer had ended. You could sense the dank smell of wormwood and wet straw in the air. What would autumn bring? For some reason I did not give it a thought.

That autumn I went back to school after a two-year break. After class I frequently went down to the river by the steep bank and sat near the old threshing shed, now silent and deserted. It was here I made my first pictures with student paints. Even then I realised my work was not without merit.

'These paints are useless,' I would say. 'If only I had some real paints.'

I had no idea what real paints were like; it was only much later that I discovered real oil paints in lead tubes. Paints or no paints, my teachers were right: I had to learn properly. But there could be no thought of learning. How could there be when we still had no word from my brothers? Anyway, my mother would never have let me go, her only son, 'the *jigit* and breadwinner of two families'. I did not dare speak about it. As if to spite me, autumn that year was so beautiful, it cried out to be painted.

The level of the icy cold Kurkureu River fell, the tops of stones at the rapids appeared, covered in dark green and orange moss. The frail, naked stems of rose-willows turned red in the early frost, yet the young poplars still retained their firm, yellow leaves.

The grimy, rain-washed tents of the herders grew black on the reddened after-grass of the flood meadow, and above the smokeholes curled ribbons of acrid blue smoke. The lean stallions whinnied loudly as they did in autumn – the mares were drifting away and it would be hard now to keep them in herds until springtime. Flocks of sheep from the hills were wandering over the stubble in little groups. The dry, windswept steppe was criss-crossed with well-trampled paths.

Soon the steppe wind began to blow, the sky grew dim and the cold rains started to fall. One fairly pleasant day I went down to the river, attracted by a fiery clump of mountain ash growing on a sandbar, and I sat down among the rose-willows just beside the ford. Evening was falling when, all of a sudden, I spotted two figures. They seemed to have just crossed the ford. It was Daniyar and Jamilia. I could not tear my gaze away from their taut, determined faces. Daniyar was walking along jerkily, a knapsack upon his shoulder, the hem of his open greatcoat flapping against the tops of his worn, tarpaulin boots. Jamilia had a white scarf tied about her head and it had slipped back; she was wearing her best print frock, the one she liked to show off on market days, and over the top a quilted corduroy jacket. In one hand she was carrying a small bundle and with the other she was holding on to a strap of Daniyar's knapsack. They were discussing something as they walked along.

Not knowing what to do, I watched them take the path through the ravine across the thicket of needlegrass. Should I give them a shout? Perhaps not.

The last crimson rays slid past the fast-moving line of skewbald clouds along the hills, and all at once it grew dark. Daniyar and Jamilia never once glanced back as they made their way towards the railway siding. A couple of times their heads bobbed in the thicket and then disappeared completely.

'Jamilia-a-a,' I cried at the top of my voice.

'A-a-a-a,' came back a forlorn echo.

'Jamilia-a-a,' I cried again, running wildly after them across the river.

Sprays of icy water splashed my face and drenched my clothes, yet I ran on oblivious of the earth beneath my feet. Then I tripped over a root and went sprawling full length. I lay there without looking up and the tears streamed down my face. Darkness seemed to be bearing down on me, the only thing I heard were the slender stems of needle-grass wailing mournfully.

'Jamilia, oh Jamilia,' I sobbed, choking on my tears.

I had parted with the two people dearest and closest

to me. And as I lay there on the ground I suddenly realized that I was in love with Jamilia. Yes, she was my first love, my childhood sweetheart.

I lay there for a long time, my head buried in my wet arm, saying farewell not only to Jamilia and Daniyar, but to my childhood.

Eventually I made my way home in the dark and came upon a great commotion in the yard: stirrups jangled as the horses were being saddled and a tipsy Orozmat pranced about on his mount, bellowing at the top of his voice.

'We should have kicked that stray mongrel out of the village ages ago. A miserable disgrace to our kin. If I ever set eyes on him again I'll kill him on the spot, I don't care if I swing for it. I won't stand for every passing tramp abducting our women. Aida, *jigits*, mount up, he won't get away, we'll intercept him at the station.'

My blood froze. Which way would the men go? As soon as I was sure they were taking the highroad to the station and not the track to the railway siding, I slipped into the house and curled into my father's sheepskin coat, covering my head so that no one saw my tears.

After that the village was filled with much talk and gossip. The women vied with one another in condemning Jamilia.

'She's a fool. Fancy leaving such a family and trampling on her happiness.'

'What on earth attracted her to him? His fortune consists only of an old greatcoat and tattered boots.'

'Well, he certainly hasn't a yard full of cattle, that's for sure. A homeless vagabond, a tramp – you can't make a silk purse out of a sow's ear. Never fear, that beauty'll come to her senses, but it'll be too late.'

'That's what I say. And what about Sadyk as a husband, what's wrong with him? The best *jigit* in the village.'

'And her mother-in-law? God doesn't grant everyone a woman like that. You'd go far to find another *baibiche* like her. She's ruined her life, the little fool, for no reason at all.'

I was probably the only one who did not condemn Jamilia, my one-time *jenei*. Maybe Daniyar did have an old greatcoat and tattered boots, but I for one knew his soul was richer than all of ours. I did not believe Jamilia would be unhappy with him, though I did feel sorry for my mother. It seemed that when Jamilia left, my mother's former strength left with her. She became stooped and haggard. Now I realize she could not accept someone breaking with tradition. If a storm uproots a mighty tree, the tree will never grow again. Earlier, my mother would never ask anyone to thread a needle for her, her pride would not allow it. One day after school I came home and saw her weeping; her hands were trembling so badly that she could not thread the needle.

'Here, you thread it,' she said with a sigh. 'Jamilia will come to no good. Ah, what a mistress she would have made for the family. Now she's gone, turned her back on us. Why did she go? Didn't she like it here?'

I wanted to hug mother and reassure her, tell her what sort of person Daniyar really was, but I did not dare for fear of offending her forever. All the same, the time soon came when my part in the affair ceased to be a secret.

Shortly after, Sadyk came back home. Naturally he was upset, though he did say once to Osman, 'Good riddance to her. She'll come to a sticky end one day. There's plenty more fish in the sea.'

'True enough,' replied Osman. 'I'm sorry I didn't catch him; I'd have slaughtered the beggar on the spot. As for her, I'd have tied her hair to my horse's tail. They probably headed south, to the cotton fields, or else to the Kazakhs, it's not the first time he's taken to the road. What I can't fathom is how it happened in the first place, without anyone knowing or suspecting a thing. The bitch fixed everything up herself. I'd give her what for if I could lay my hands on her.'

Listening to such bold talk I felt like telling Osman, 'You can't forget her rejecting you in the haystack. What a mean streak you have.'

One day as I sat at home drawing a sketch for the school paper, and mother fussed about in the kitchen, Sadyk abruptly burst into the room. He was pale and his eyes glinted angrily as he thrust a sheet of paper in my face.

'Did you do this?'

I was dumbstruck. It was my first drawing. At that moment Daniyar and Jamilia seemed to come alive as they stared at me.

'I did.'

'Who's this?' he said poking a finger at the paper.

'Daniyar.'

'Traitor,' he hissed.

He ripped the drawing to bits and went out, slamming the door behind him.

After a lengthy, oppressive silence, my mother asked, 'You knew?'

'Yes.'

Leaning against the stove, she stared at me with such reproach and incomprehension. And when I said, 'I'd draw them again too,' she shook her head sadly and helplessly.

Meanwhile, as I looked at the pieces of paper scattered over the floor, an unbearable pain welled up inside me. Let them brand me a traitor. Whom had I betrayed? The family? Our kin? But I had not betrayed the truth, the truth of life, the truth of those two people. I could not tell anyone about them, even my mother would not understand.

Everything swam before my eyes, the bits of paper seemed to come alive and swirl about the floor. The memory of Daniyar and Jamilia gazing at me from the drawing was so vivid; I imagined in that instant that I could hear the song Daniyar had sung that memorable August night. I remembered them leaving the village, and within me came an irresistible urge to take to the road, to leave like them, boldly and resolutely, taking the hard road to happiness.

'I'll go away and study,' I told my mother. 'Tell father. I want to be an artist.'

I felt sure she would try to stop me, start to cry and remind me of my brothers who had died in the war. To my surprise, however, she did not cry, she just said sadly and softly,

'Go on then. You've all grown feathers and fluttered your wings in your own way. How are we to know how high you'll fly? Maybe you're right. Go on then. Or maybe you'll change your mind when you get there. It's no trade, you know, drawing and painting things. You'll live and learn. But don't forget your own home.'

From that day on the Little House separated from us. Soon after, I left home to study.

That's the story.

I presented my diploma work at the academy where I went directly from art school: it was the picture I had long dreamed of. It is not hard to guess it was a painting of Daniyar and Jamilia walking along the autumn steppe road with a broad, bright expanse before them.

Maybe my painting is not perfect – perfection does not come readily to the artist – but it is immensely dear to me, for it was my first conscious creation.

There are times when I am dissatisfied with my work, there are troublesome moments when I lose faith in myself. At such times I am drawn to this painting that means so much to me, to Daniyar and Jamilia. I gaze at them for a long time, and I talk to them.

Where are you now? What roads are you treading? We have so many new roads now, right across the steppe all the way to the Altai and Siberia. Many brave souls are toiling there. Perhaps you're among them? You left, my Jamilia, across the wide steppe without a backward glance. Perhaps you are weary, perhaps you have lost faith in yourself? Just lean on Daniyar's shoulder. Have him sing to you his song of love, of life, of the earth. May the steppe come alive and blossom in all its glory. May you recall that August night. Keep on, Jamilia, have no regrets; you've found your hard-sought happiness.

When I gaze at them long enough I can hear Daniyar's voice. He is calling to me, too, to take the highroad, which means it is time for me to get ready. I shall cross the steppe back to my village and find fresh colours there.

May Daniyar's song resound and may Jamilia's heart beat with every stroke of my brush.